FLY GUY'S BIG FAMILY

Tedd Arnold

Cartwheel Books

An Imprint of Scholastic Inc.

For Louise and Steve and the big Brown family!

Copyright © 2017 by Tedd Arnold

All rights reserved. Published by Scholastic Inc., *Publishers since 1920*. SCHOLASTIC, CARTWHEEL BOOKS, and associated logos are trademarks and/or registered trademarks of Scholastic Inc.

The publisher does not have any control over and does not assume any responsibility for author or third-party websites or their content.

No part of this publication may be reproduced, stored in a retrieval system, or transmitted in any form or by any means, electronic, mechanical, photocopying, recording, or otherwise, without written permission of the publisher. For information regarding permission, write to Scholastic Inc., Attention: Permissions Department, 557 Broadway, New York, NY 10012.

Library of Congress Cataloging-in-Publication Data available
ISBN 978-0-545-66316-8

10 9 8 7 6 5 4 3 2 1   17 18 19 20 21

Printed in China   38
First edition, September 2017
Book design by Steve Ponzo

A boy had a pet fly.
He named him Fly Guy.
Fly Guy could say the
boy's name—

Chapter 1

Buzz wanted to play.
He looked for Fly Guy.
"There you are," said Buzz.
"What are you doing?"

"Oh, you are drawing pictures
of your family," said Buzz.

"I bet you miss them,"
said Buzz.
"I do," said Fly Guy.
Buzz had a plan.

He secretly made little signs
with pictures of Fly Guy.

He put signs up around his
neighborhood.

Buzz made a special phone call.

Then he waited at the front door.

Chapter 2

A fly flew up to Buzz.
"Who are you?" said Buzz.

"You're Fly Guy's cousin?"
asked Buzz.

"YEZZ!" said the fly.

"Cool," said Buzz. "Come in!"

The fly looked worried.

"No fly swatters," said Buzz.
"It is safe here!"

Fly Guy's cousin turned
and called out—

Thousands of flies came out from hiding. They all flew into the house.

"Wow!" said Buzz. "Flies have big families!"

Outside his bedroom, Buzz said, "Sh-h-h-h-h!"

He opened the door and said, "Fly Guy, it's time for dinner."

Fly Guy flew out.

Fly Guy was very surprised!

He hugged his cousin.

He hugged another cousin.

He hugged another cousin.

Chapter 3

After Fly Guy hugged his whole family, Buzz said, "It really is time for dinner. Everyone follow me!"

Buzz, Fly Guy, and all the flies came to the table.

Mom and Dad were surprised. "What are we going to do with all these flies?" cried Dad.

"Don't worry," said Buzz.
"They are Fly Guy's family
and I made a plan."

Buzz opened the window.
"TIME TO PARTY!"

Outside, a truck dumped garbage in the yard and drove away.

Fly Guy and his family flew
outside.

They had a party in the garbage!

Fly Guy's mom and dad brought something for him to see.

After everyone went home, Buzz said, "Great party! Were you surprised?"

"Here," said Buzz, "is another little surprise. Your drawings!"